Penelope Snoop

ACE DETECTIVE

For Albie and his cats, Bear and Carlos. Love Mummy x - P.B.

To Achille and Colette and all their magical adventures - C.R.

BLOOMSBURY CHILDREN'S BOOKS
Bloomsbury Publishing Plc
50 Bedford Square, London, WC1B 3DP, UK
29 Earlsfort Terrace, Dublin 2, Ireland

BLOOMSBURY, BLOOMSBURY CHILDREN'S BOOKS and the Diana logo are trademarks of Bloomsbury Publishing Plc
First published in Great Britain 2022 by Bloomsbury Publishing Plc

A catalogue record for this book is available from the British Library

ISBN HB: 978 1 4088 5693 2
ISBN PB: 978 1 4088 5695 6
ISBN eBook: 978 1 4088 5694 9

2 4 6 8 10 9 7 5 3 1

Printed and bound in China by Leo Paper Products, Heshan, Guangdong

To find out more about our authors and books visit www.bloomsbury.com and sign up for our newsletters

Penelope Snoop
ACE DETECTIVE

WRITTEN BY
Pamela Butchart

ILLUSTRATED BY
Christine Roussey

BLOOMSBURY
CHILDREN'S BOOKS
LONDON OXFORD NEW YORK NEW DELHI SYDNEY

Penelope Snoop was the BEST Finder-Outer-in-the-Whole-Wide-World.

After all, with her trusty DOG, *Carlos*, she had:

1. **CRACKED** the Case of the Curious Croaking

2. ***SOLVED*** the Mystery of the Missing Homework

3. **DISCOVERED** Dad's Disappearing Chocolate

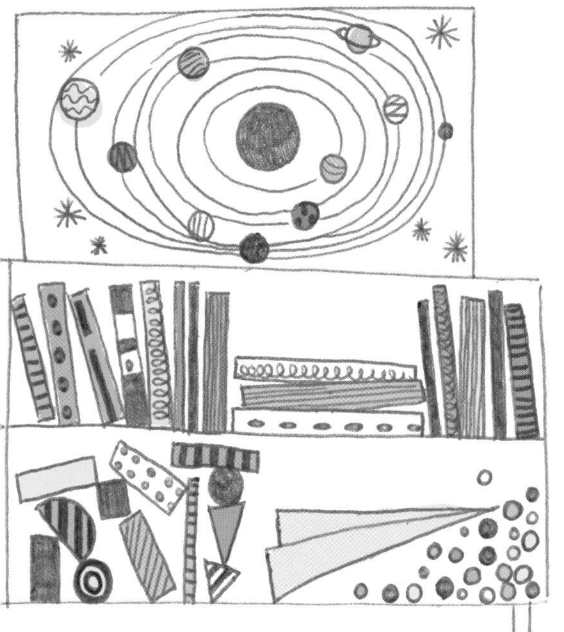

But today she had an even **BIGGER CASE** to solve . . .

Sidney the Smelly Sock Snake had

DISAPPEARED!

She COULDN'T find him anywhere.

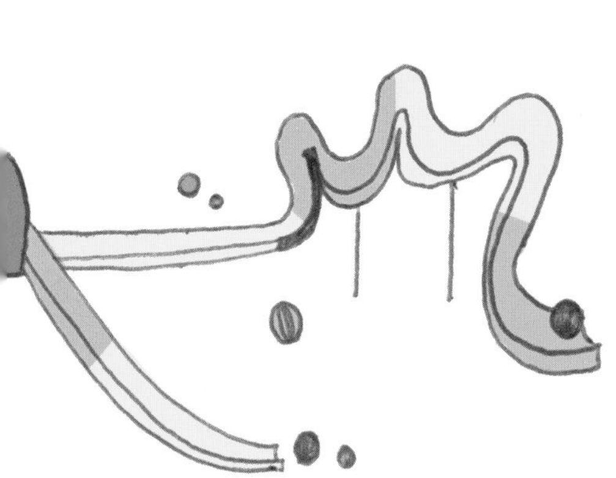

Sidney had DEFINITELY been in her bed when she woke up that morning – because she remembered *WIPING* dribble from his face.

And he had DEFINITELY sat on her knee when she ATE her breakfast – because she remembered DROPPING some *runny* egg yolk on his head.

And there was NO DOUBT he was sitting on the bath stool when she was *CLEANING* her TEETH (because she remembered making funny faces at him in the mirror).

BUT WHERE WAS HE NOW?

There was NO DOUBT about it. *Sidney* the Smelly Sock Snake had been . . .

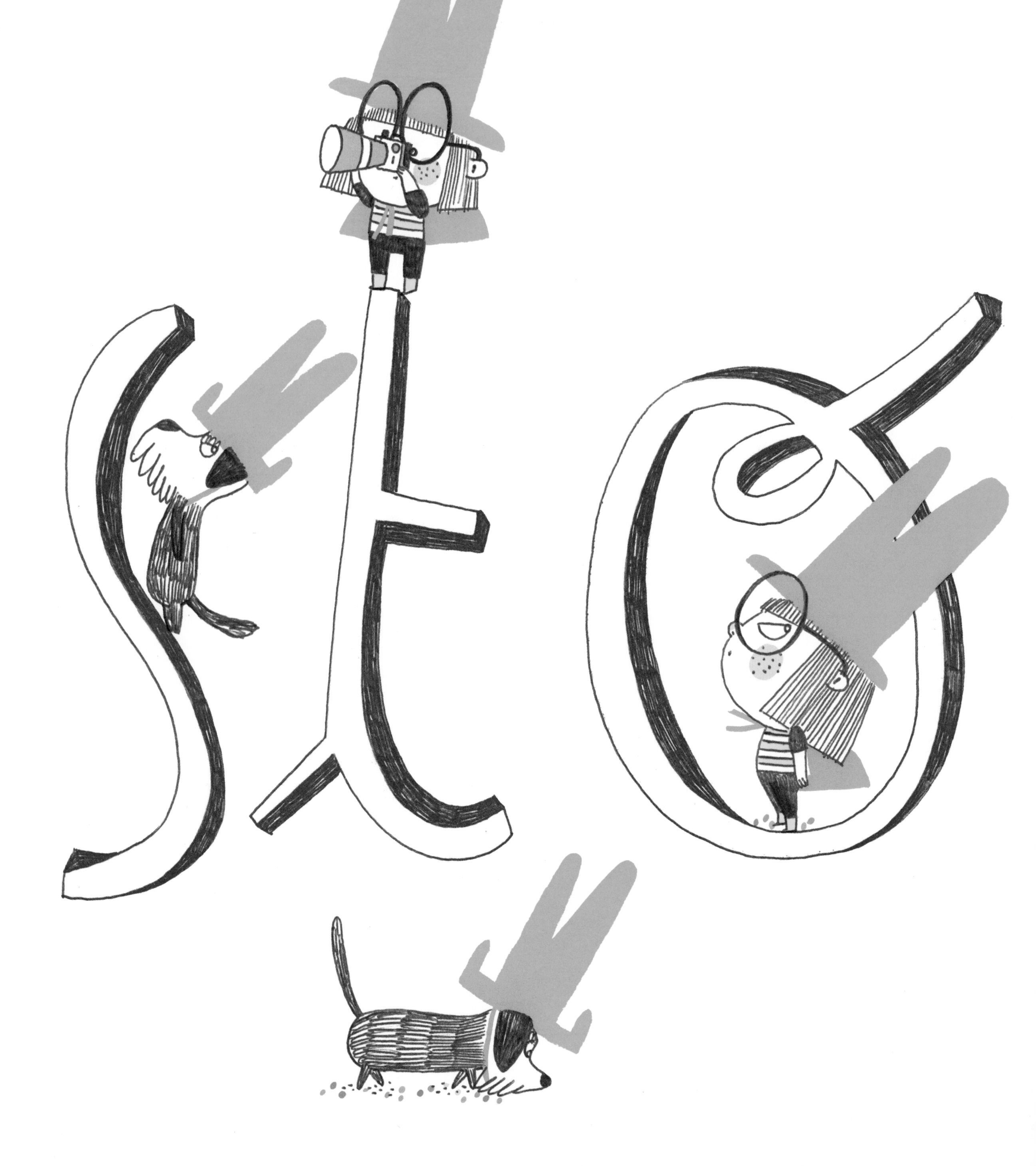
sto

lem!

Penelope Snoop and her SLEUTHING sidekick ran into the kitchen. The fridge was making its weird *WHIRRING* noise, which ALWAYS meant . . .

something SERIOUSLY SUSPICIOUS was going on.

The ACE Detective ran to her SUPER-SECRET hiding place and dug out her FINDER-OUTER KIT.

Carlos DIDN'T like wearing his hat very much but Penelope Snoop insisted because this was a SERIOUS investigation.

The CASE of the STOLEN Sock Snake was **OFFICIALLY** OPEN.

Penelope Snoop and *Carlos* decided that outside would be the place to **EXPLORE** first.

So they JUMPED onto the SUPER-TRANSPORTER
and rode ALL THE WAY to the back garden.

And THAT'S when they found
their first **CLUE** . . .

. . . a GIANT muddy footprint.

There was NO doubt about it. *Sidney* the Smelly Sock Snake had been STOLEN by a squelchy mud monster!

"Hello Mr Frog," said Penelope Snoop.
"Have YOU seen a mud monster today?"
But the frog fountain just
STARED at them.

So Penelope Snoop STARED right back until
that frog decided to be HELPFUL.

"What's that? You SAW something
SUSPICIOUS in the tree house?"
she said.

So Penelope Snoop and Carlos
SWAM all the way
across the garden . . .

and climbed up
ONE HUNDRED
stairs
until they
reached the
tree house.

"We KNOW you're in there, Mr Mud Monster."
"We have you TRAPPED and surrounded by sharks so you better give Sidney back RIGHT NOW!"

But there was NO mud monster inside.

"That mud monster must've kidnapped Sidney and taken him to Mud Monster MOON!" cried Penelope Snoop.

"Come on, Carlos. Let's take the Super SPACE-BLASTER."

But the moon was
completely EMPTY!

"Where could he BE, Carlos?"
said Penelope Snoop.

She took out her SUPER-STRENGTH TELESCOPE and peered back at Planet Earth.

And that's when she spotted a DARK SHADOW in the kitchen.

"That mud monster tricked us!" said Penelope Snoop.
"He's been hiding in the KITCHEN all along."

Penelope Snoop and Carlos *WHIZZED* back to the treehouse . . .

RACED down ONE HUNDRED stairs . . .

SWAM across the grassy sea . . .

JUMPED on the SUPER-TRANSPORTER . . .

and rode

ALL THE WAY

home.

And THAT'S when *Penelope Snoop*

noticed a TRAIL of muddy footprints . . .

that led **ALL THE WAY** to . . .

. . . her **MUM'S** wellies!

"You're **NOT** a mud monster!"

cried *Penelope Snoop*.

"You're **MUM**!"

"It was **YOUR** muddy footprint we found by the frog fountain.

And it was **YOU** who **STOLE** *Sidney*!"

"I'm sorry," said Mum.
"I just wanted to give him a
LITTLE wash. He was a bit more
whiffy than usual."
And THEN Penelope Snoop noticed . . .

. . . THE WASHING MACHINE!

Poor Sidney the Smelly Sock Snake!

"That's ANOTHER mystery solved, Carlos!" said Penelope Snoop, giving Sidney a big squeeze.

"Until NEXT time . . ."